Sophie Bakes a Cake

Tina Burke

PENGUIN | VIKING

Sophie and Scarlett
were helping to bake a cake.

Everything was ready.

Sophie stirred the flour, sugar, butter, milk, and one egg.

Scarlett thought it
needed some peanut butter,

so Sophie added it.

Scarlett thought it
needed some Vegemite,

so Sophie added it.

Scarlett thought it needed a crayon,

so Sophie added it.

Mum put the mixture into the oven, and Sophie and Scarlett waited...

and waited.

When it was ready,
Sophie gave some to Scarlett,

and some to herself.

Scarlett thought it was delicious.

So Sophie gave Scarlett her piece, too.

VIKING

Published by the Penguin Group
Penguin Group (Australia)
250 Camberwell Road, Camberwell, Victoria 3124, Australia
(a division of Pearson Australia Group Pty Ltd)
Penguin Group (USA) Inc.
375 Hudson Street, New York, New York 10014, USA
Penguin Group (Canada)
90 Eglinton Avenue East, Suite 700, Toronto, Canada ON M4P 2Y3
(a division of Pearson Penguin Canada Inc.)
Penguin Books Ltd
80 Strand, London WC2R 0RL England
Penguin Ireland
25 St Stephen's Green, Dublin 2, Ireland
(a division of Penguin Books Ltd)
Penguin Books India Pvt Ltd
11 Community Centre, Panchsheel Park, New Delhi – 110 017, India
Penguin Group (NZ)
67 Apollo Drive, Rosedale, North Shore 0632, New Zealand
(a division of Pearson New Zealand Ltd)
Penguin Books (South Africa) (Pty) Ltd
24 Sturdee Avenue, Rosebank, Johannesburg 2196, South Africa

Penguin Books Ltd, Registered Offices: 80 Strand, London, WC2R 0RL, England

First published by Penguin Group (Australia), 2008

1 3 5 7 9 10 8 6 4 2

Text and illustration copyright © Tina Burke, 2008

The moral right of the author has been asserted.

Cover and text design by Karen Trump © Penguin Group (Australia)
Printed in China by 1010 Printing International Limited

National Library of Australia
Cataloguing-in-Publication data:

Burke, Tina
Sophie bakes a cake

ISBN: 978 0 67 007279 8

I.Title

A823.4

puffin.com.au